What Horses Do After Racing

The Story of Good Carma

Jay Privman

REDCLIFF
PUBLISHING

©2024 by Jay Privman

All rights reserved.

No part of this publication may be reproduced or transmitted in any form or by any means, electronic or mechanical, including photography, recording, or any information storage and retrieval system, without permission in writing from the author. For permission requests, visit www.carma4horses.org

Published by Redcliff Publishing
California, USA

What Horses do After Racing: The Story of Good Carma

978-1-7367095-8-0 PAPERBACK
978-1-7367095-9-7 HARDCOVER

DEDICATION

To every thoroughbred racehorse who has charged down the track, may you have the same love and joy in retirement that you brought to fans in every race.

FOREWORD

A lifetime of being around horses has not only shown me their remarkable abilities, but also the profound connections they can form with us. This understanding drew me to the work of aftercare—the next chapters in the lives of racehorses. **CARMA**, *a 501(c3) charitable organization, works with farms and ranches to retrain racehorses for their new careers, such as show jumping, dressage, and trail riding. Some will also go on to do the very impactful work of serving as therapy horses.*

I was deeply moved by a colleague's autistic sons who were captivated by horses. That, and just believing that horses who give us so much pleasure deserve a proper post-racing career, are what brought me to **CARMA** *and, in turn, to this book project.*

On average, horses can live to age 20 or more, but they only race, with rare exceptions, through ages 5-8. So, their post-race life is often longer than their racing life. That is why aftercare is so important. It provides a way for horses to transition to the next phase of their lives, offering them new opportunities and enriching the lives of the people they touch.

— Jay Privman

ACKNOWLEDGMENTS

We would like to express our heartfelt thanks to everyone who has made this book possible and supported our mission to ensure a bright future for retired racehorses. Foremost, we are immensely thankful to all **CARMA** donors; your generosity fuels our ability to make a real and lasting difference for our big-hearted athletes.

A special thank you to **Christine Siegel** and the team at **PM Advertising** for the art work that brings the vibrant story within these pages to life with creativity and passion.

Our gratitude extends to the dedicated members of the CARMA Board of Directors and Founders, past and present— including the late **Mace Siegel** and **Howard "Howie" Zucker**—whose guidance and support are the backbone of our success.

Thank you for your support and for being part of this important journey.

Good Carma is a beautiful filly, a girl horse.
She is chestnut-colored, shiny like a copper penny, with
a generous splash of white cascading down her face, and white
on the bottom of her legs, making it look like she's wearing socks!

She used to be a racehorse. She loved to race. The fans loved to watch her compete, and all her horsey friends at the track watched her with admiration because of her success.

She never won a major race like the Kentucky Derby, but she won a lot of races. Her friends in the barn of her trainer, **Mr. Drew**, were race winners, too. There was **Lovely Lucinda**, another filly, and her filly friend, **Stylish Samantha**. And the bad boy colt of the bunch, **Silly Billy**. They loved being around one another at the track.

But eventually their racing careers came to an end, and it was time to move on to do something else. One night, after **Mr. Drew** went home and turned out the lights, the four of them stuck their heads out of their stalls at the barn and talked about where they'd like to go next.

"I want to do dressage. It's like horse ballet. I can get my hair all done up, have a rider on my back who also looks pretty, and move around like a ballerina," **Stylish Samantha** said.

"Dressage is too slow for me. I'm high energy. I like to go fast and jump over things. I can't wait to be a hunter-jumper," said **Silly Billy**. "But just getting turned out and running around in a field sounds fun to me, too! Either way, I'll be OK."

"I'd like to go on trail rides. Just take it nice and easy, enjoy nature. Pay attention to the birds and the flowers," said **Lovely Lucinda.**

Finally, **Good Carma** spoke up. "So many great choices! As for me, I want to be a therapy horse. So many people benefit by being around horses to help them achieve their goals, and I want to help them."

When **Mr. Drew** came to the barn the next morning,
all four horses told him what they'd like to do next.
Mr. Drew knew just who to call.

His friend, **Miss Madeline**, had started a charity that helps former racehorses make the transition to second careers, just like **Good Carma**, **Stylish Samantha**, **Lovely Lucinda**, and **Silly Billy** were hoping to do.

Miss Madeline's charity is **CARMA**, which stands for California Retirement Management Account. People who own horses, train horses, regular fans — anyone who loves horses — can donate money to **CARMA**. **CARMA** grants that money to farms and training centers that specialize in helping racehorses learn their new careers.

"That's how **Good Carma** got her name," **Miss Madeline** said. "Her owner, **Miss Amy**, thought it was a fun play on words. It's good karma to give to **CARMA**!"

Miss Madeline found all of them a new home. **Stylish Samantha** went to a training center where she was taught how to pose like a ballerina.

Silly Billy learned how to jump over obstacles so he could compete as a hunter-jumper.

Lovely Lucinda stopped to smell the roses. She never ran in the Kentucky Derby, which is known as the Run for the Roses, so she called her trail rides the Walk for the Roses!

And **Good Carma** went to a ranch where children with special needs, and military veterans, benefitted from bonding with a kind-hearted animal like **Good Carma**.

All four of them had had fun careers as racehorses. And all found their way to doing something equally rewarding and worthwhile when they were done racing, thanks to **CARMA**.

HELP HORSES LIKE GOOD CARMA & FRIENDS

Join us in supporting **CARMA** as we find new homes for retired racehorses like **Good Carma**, **Stylish Samantha**, **Lovely Lucinda**, and **Silly Billy** and enrich communities through our aftercare charity partners. Many of these aftercare organizations go beyond just offering safe havens for horses—they provide crucial community services such as volunteer opportunities, equine education, and therapeutic programs that help both people and horses.

By donating to **CARMA**, you're helping ensure that beloved Thoroughbreds enjoy a fulfilling retirement, and you're supporting valuable resources that bring education, healing, and joy to our communities.

Donate today at carma4horses.org

Interested in adopting an off-the-track Thoroughbred?
Check out our network of approved Aftercare Charities:
carma4horses.org/aftercare_charities

Jay Privman won numerous awards covering horse racing for more than 40 years for publications such as Daily Racing Form and The New York Times, and as a racing reporter for CBS, ESPN, Fox, and NBC. He covered the Kentucky Derby 39 times. He also serves as a current **CARMA** Board member. He and his wife Anne Warner live near Del Mar racetrack in Southern California. He has eight grandchildren, and they provided the inspirational tone for this book.

CARMA is a 501(c3) non-profit organization dedicated to the aftercare of Thoroughbreds retiring from racing. **CARMA** focuses on raising awareness and providing educational resources about equine retirement to both the public and the racing community. By facilitating the smooth transition of retiring racehorses into new homes and second careers, **CARMA** ensures that California-raced Thoroughbreds have a secure and fulfilling life after racing.

Since its inception in 2007, **CARMA** has successfully placed over 425 Thoroughbreds through its Placement Program, and has distributed more than $5.8 million in grants to reputable Aftercare Charity Partners, profoundly impacting the lives of countless equine athletes. All donations to **CARMA** are tax-deductible. Tax ID #80-0146395

Learn More & Donate: **CARMA4HORSES.ORG**